THE MONARCH'S DREAM

Chief Manana's Wake-up Call to Africa

by

Simon J. Nkanda

DORRANCE PUBLISHING CO., INC.
PITTSBURGH, PENNSYLVANIA 15222

ISBN # 0-8059-6354-5
Printed in the United States of America

First Printing

For information or to order additional books, please write:
Dorrance Publishing Co., Inc.
701 Smithfield Street
Third Floor
Pittsburgh, Pennsylvania 15222
U.S.A.
1-800-788-7654
Or visit our web site and on-line catalog at
www. dorrancepublishing.com

Dedication

This short story is dedicated to my son, Sabo Thornton Nkanda, for without my love for him I could not have found a source of inspiration and courage to paint the kind of mental picture as depicted in the story. Although he is not a prince in the conventional sense, Sabo (meaning "treasure") represents, in my life, the attributes of love reflected in the story. In a sense, he is a prince in his own right.

Contents

Foreword

The Monarch's Dream: Chief Manana's Wake-up Call to Africa is a fictional story based on personal experiences and the general reading material referenced at the end of the story. The characters featured in the story are not people I knew in real life, nor is the place, Izumba. It is, however, not uncommon to find such names in different parts of Africa bonafide to real people and perhaps a locale named Izumba.

My concept of the story is drawn from similar situations and experiences that at some point in my life were prevalent in the eastern part of Africa, such as the chiefdoms that existed during the colonial era as forms of local government. In particular, my experiences were accentuated by one occasion when, as a young boy, my father took me with him to visit the local chief, who happened to be a distant relative. Nonetheless, the name used in the story does not refer to the chief I visited.

It is my hope that the story will be interesting if not amusing enough to conjure the essence and meaning of the different scenarios presented, thus the need to read the story in its entirety. Focal to the story is the speech presented by the character portrayed as the "Prince."

CHAPTER 1

Chief Manana

Before the time of political independence among African countries in the early sixties, chiefdoms had been a prevalent form of traditional government. Chiefs were highly regarded and treated with extraordinary dignity. They symbolized power, authority, and great eminence within social structures. Despite the existence of colonial rule, these leaders had the loyalty and genuine love of the people under their jurisdiction. Embedded in their lifestyle were the fundamental values of African culture–extended family, sharing, and compassion toward the elderly. It was among these exceptional men that we find Chief Manana of Izumba, a small chiefdom in the grasslands of eastern Africa.

For many years the land of Izumba had enjoyed peace and tranquillity under the leadership of Chief Manana in the midst of colonial rule. Copious harvests, green pastures, and cordial neighborliness were commonplace in Chief Manana's domain. The chief, who had ruled Izumba for nearly four decades, often prided himself on the prospects of his land and his sizable family of four wives and twelve children. He was, indeed, a paramount member of this unique community.

At the age of seventy, however, Chief Manana had begun to feel that he had accomplished enough for his people and his family, that it was appropriate to appoint and groom an heir in readiness for the throne when he could no longer rule effectively. On the face of it one would imagine that unless Chief Manana followed the long-held tradition of promoting the first-born son to his first wife, he would have a difficult time deciding who his heir was to be, given the number of children he had.

However, in Chief Manana's mind that was not the case. For many years he had known who the heir would be, but had not disclosed his secret to anyone in his family nor to the community at large. In his mind, there was no doubt that Mbesi, the first-born child to his second wife, was going to become the heir to his throne. He was fully cognizant, nonetheless, of the fact that a measure like this would stir much controversy in relation to the traditional norm of passing the throne to the first wife's first-born son. Chief Manana would be the first one in the known history of the community to appoint an heir from a second wife instead of the first.

In his mind, the chief believed that Mbesi was his mirror image; intelligent, witty, and handsome, just like himself. "I shall renew myself through Mbesi, and my rule shall continue unchanged," he had convinced himself. In many respects, there seemed to be some underlying truth in the chief's view of his son Mbesi. For even among members of the community, Mbesi commanded the highest honor and respect compared to many youths among his age group and in particular, his many half-brothers. He had outstanding academic and athletic abilities and was always thorough and committed to everything he undertook.

Despite his royal status, Mbesi was known to have a boundless reach for friendship and generosity. It was not uncommon to hear from time to time from among members of the surrounding communities a story of kindness, charity, or heroics of some sort told about him. It was much to his praise and honor, for example, when once a young teenager about his age confessed before a gathering how Mbesi had come to his rescue when a group of fellow playmates nearly attacked him for losing the only *pia* (a cone-shaped object used in a game similar to golf) they had and spoiling the game. As the group began pushing him around and calling him names, Mbesi, who was returning from track practice, spotted the commotion and ran to intervene despite the advice of the royal service staff who often accompanied him to various events. He risked his own safety for someone he hardly knew. The group dispersed as they saw Mbesi approaching, calling a stern warning of serious reprisal to anyone who would cause harm to the young man.

On the contrary, his half-brother, the first-born to Chief Manana's first wife, was more of a reserved individual who paid little attention to public common affairs. Not driven to formal academic challenges nor athleticism, instead he was pragmatic, self-taught, and preoccupied with family wealth and the pleasures that life had to offer, something his father was keenly aware of. His position in the family structure, however, was well respected. Much responsibility lay in his hands regarding farming, cattle auction, and transportation operations. He oversaw what came into the family treasury and made sure nothing was given away for no return. He was the iron hand for the royal family and his father respected him for his virtues. Yet, despite the strong characteristics Tunge possessed, Chief Manana had reservations about his heir apparent being a leader of the people of Izumba. His futuristic view of Izumba went beyond tradition or mere conventional character.

A day was to come, therefore, when Chief Manana would call Mbesi to tell him his most guarded secret that had never been disclosed to anyone before, not to the chief's wives nor the monarch's inner circle. Mbesi was in for a big surprise as he never had the slightest idea of what was about to be handed to him. The young man, who had just turned eighteen, was for most of his time devoted to his academic and athletic activities, although needless to say loyal to his father. When called, Mbesi was always willing to do what his father asked him to do, something that made the chief a very proud father. Besides, Mbesi was now an accomplished warrior as he had been through his "Right of Passage" ritual and stepped into manhood. Also, adding to his overflowing cup of achievements was a trophy for winning first place in track and javelin. All these attributes contributed to his father's assurance that he was making the right choice for an heir to the throne.

The preparation for the father and son meeting was to be thorough. Orders were given to ensure that all routine occurrences were suspended and that there would be no interruption while the meeting was in progress. A select staff from Royal Protocol was to be charged with the duty of ensuring that everything went according to plans. The meeting would take place in the chief's most sacred chamber, where only special ceremonies were conducted. It would be one of those few days in a year that a special drink would be served. This was going to be the day of internal transfer of power.

CHAPTER 2

The Meeting

It was not until everything was well in order, just like the chief wanted it, that the word was sent to Mbesi. The head of protocol, who was among the select staff involved with the process, was called in and instructed to deliver the word to the soon-to-be "Prince."

"I want you to go and find Mbesi," the chief began, his hands cupped together and thumbs rubbing against each other. "If you find him reading his books or doing something pertaining to his schoolwork, do not disturb him. Let him finish and then respectfully approach him. As you begin to speak to him, greet him with a word of honor, then deliver the message. Tell my son that tomorrow at three o'clock I must have a meeting with him in my special chamber, where preparations have been made. He must wear his warrior attire to the meeting. You and your staff will escort him to the special chamber."

"Your Highness," the head of protocol interrupted as the chief paused, "this is quite an honor but I must ask a question, with your permission."

"You have my permission, although I sense that you are trying to read my mind so you can find reason to oppose me," the chief remarked.

"No, Your Highness. My question is simply out of sheer curiosity. . . . You see, for the last two days I couldn't help noticing that preparations of the sacred chamber were not what I would call mundane. Rather they were pointing to something exceptionally special and now, to know that this was for Mbesi, would it be accurate to assume that Master Mbesi is about to be Prince Mbesi?"

"I can understand your curiosity, but at this point your thoughts should not establish any notion in the minds of others. You must refrain from speculation. The time will come when everything will be made clear to everyone, and if there is truth in your present thoughts then you will be the one to reaffirm your power of prediction. Now you must adhere to the instructions I have given you," the chief sternly commanded.

"But, pardon me, Your Highness," the head of protocol said, bending on his knees, "your words of wisdom must always take precedence. However, if I may stand on my nebulous ground as a member of your advisory council, I would like to offer a piece of advice, should my predictions be correct."

"And what is your piece of advice?" the chief asked rhetorically.

"Your Highness, this dominion, as we all know, has been the strongest, most prosperous, and most peaceful among all dominions around. . . . And it has been so because of the manner in which the throne has been passed on to the next generation. I am talking about the first-born son to the first mother of the land. It is my strongest conviction that the spirits of our ancestors have always embraced this tradition and to digress from it may offend the spirits and ultimately lead to a path of destruction. Your Highness, the people of this dominion expect that the throne will be passed on to the young generation in the same manner it has always been. There is no doubt in my mind that if Master Mbesi is to be your successor, it would be an unbearable burden upon you, the royal family, and above all, Master Mbesi, to have to account for the departure from a tradition known since time immemorial. I know that I may be dipping my own body and soul into a pond of salt water by uttering these words before you, but should there be a trace of truth in my rambling thoughts, I beg you, Your Highness, to spare me and take time to ponder."

"Your words of advice are very profound. I must admit I had underestimated your loyalty to tradition. However, it is unfortunate that any decision of mine will not be turned by one member of the advisory council. You know that it is the tradition of this dominion to advise the throne by consensus view of that advisory council. You may have thought well, but you did not complete your homework, and I will avoid the speculation that you presented your thoughts on your own to earn a little credibility over the council. With that in mind I shall assume that you will carry out the order I gave you without any reservations." Chief Manana was dead serious. His words resonated with authority and it was evident that the chief of protocol was better off remaining silent on the subject lest he fell out of favor with royalty.

"You must now leave, go and find Mbesi, and make sure he is prepared for the meeting in the manner I instructed you."

"Consider your orders fulfilled, Your Highness," the chief of protocol said while bowing as a gesture to leave.

As he walked down past the royal garden, Saaka, the chief of protocol, looked deeply perturbed. One could tell there was a look of fear on his face, the fear that he might have put his position in the royal ranks in jeopardy. Secondly, there was the expression of doubt on his face, because he was unsure Chief Manana was making the right decision in grooming Mbesi as future Chief of Izumba. But despite these odds, he had orders to carry out, so at this time he was headed for Mbesi's private quarters. Traditionally in Izumba, as it is in many African cultures, a young man of eighteen years must have his own quarters for his privacy. It is a shameful thing for a young man of this age to share living quarters with parents.

"Ikeja-a-a!" he yelled at one of the royal service staff who had just finished his day's chores. "Come here, quick! I want you to go and fetch Master Mbesi's warrior attire. Prepare it for him for tomorrow. I shall tell you exactly what time to bring it to his quarters. In the meantime, you are not to tell anyone about this. Understood?"

"Yes, sir," replied Ikeja.

"Now, go!"

Saaka proceeded toward Mbesi's quarters but as he was halfway across the royal compound, he suddenly stopped, his index finger against his lips. He appeared to have remembered something and was pondering over it. He then turned around and began walking toward his own quarters, taking a shortcut across the garden. He had remembered Chief Manana's instructions: "If you find him occupied with his schoolwork, you must not disturb him." Therefore he thought it was possible Mbesi may have been reading as he was fond of reading whenever he was in his quarters until it was time for supper. At the same time, Saaka remembered that Mbesi was always an ardent lover of the evening gathering in the royal social square where all the young men in the royal compound got together to listen to storytellers who told various tales of bravery, humor, and fortune. Saaka knew that this was something Mbesi never missed attending and knowing that it was going to take place that evening, he decided to wait until it was almost time for Mbesi to go to the social square. He would then go to Mbesi's quarters to deliver the message and have the opportunity to walk with the soon-to-be prince to the social gathering.

The social event was to begin shortly after sunset. At this time all the young men within the royal compound and friends from nearby were gathered, eagerly waiting for the storyteller to arrive. Mbesi, who was an avid fan of the occasion, had put his books away an hour earlier and had got himself ready to leave his quarters when suddenly the chief of protocol showed up at his gate. It seemed rather unusual and for a moment Mbesi was startled. He stood motionless just a few yards from his doorstep as he saw Saaka standing by the gate with a look of someone with a serious message to deliver. "Oh! Well, Saaka, I didn't expect you. . . . What brings you here at this hour? Is everything all right? Did Father send you to tell me something? You know tonight is a social night at the square!" he spoke frantically.

"It's okay, Master Mbesi. I see you are all set for the evening. The young men are already gathered; I saw them as I was coming here. I am sorry for my unexpected visit, I should have done it at a more convenient time. But you should not worry, I am not here to bring bad news."

"Good!" Mbesi shouted, his face gleaming with a smile. "Now you can walk with me down to the square and tell me what you have to say. But before you say anything, I want you to know that I really appreciate your loyalty to my father and my family, and let me tell you, if my father were to put me in a high position after my schooling, I'll make sure you and your family are well taken care of."

"Oh, that's very kind of you, Master Mbesi . . . but–" the chief of protocol said rather impatiently.

"No, I mean it!" Mbesi cut him short. "You see, I know that I do not stand a chance of becoming my father's successor–that's my brother's right–but with my education, my brother will always make sure I am close to him for advice and direction on matters that affect the economy and peace of our land."

By this time the two were nearly halfway to the square and Saaka was getting anxious to deliver the message. "You know, Master Mbesi, I have always wished you success in your school work. . . . Now, let me not rob you of your time for the entertainment that's about to begin." Saaka deliberately slowed down to a near stop to make sure the message was properly delivered.

"Master Mbesi," Saaka began, his hands cupped together and his head slightly bowed, "this afternoon I was called by your father and asked to deliver this message to you: Tomorrow at three o'clock, your father would like to have a meeting with you in the special chamber where he holds meetings with dignitaries and the advisory council. You are to come to the meeting dressed in your warrior attire. I have assigned a member of the royal service staff to have your attire prepared for you tomorrow. It will be brought to you earlier in the day and I will have the honor to escort you to the meeting. I am fully aware that it will not be a meeting involving bad news, so you need not worry."

Mbesi was speechless for a moment. "Then. . . . How can you be so sure? Did my father tell you what it was all about?"

"Master Mbesi, you can trust me that it's nothing to worry about. Your father assured me it is going to be nothing but good substance."

"Well, Saaka, you have done your duty. I'll look forward to seeing you tomorrow before three o'clock.

The two men were now at the royal social square where the crowd was increasingly growing. It was time for Mbesi to put the news in the back of his mind and allow himself to enjoy the evening. "Master Mbesi, I hope you have an enjoyable evening. I have to go now."

But as Saaka bowed and turned around to leave, his son, who was a good friend of Mbesi, arrived and was excited to see his friend, whom he had not seen since their track meet a week earlier. "Father, I wondered where you were! Are you going to join us tonight? I think you need to, because your favorite village poetry singer, Inoni, (or the big bird,) will be here to kick off the event."

"Ioni is here tonight?"

"Yes, sir."

"Well, that makes me want to intrude on this youngster gathering."

"I'm sure you will have fun, at least for that part of it," Mbesi remarked.

Meanwhile the crowd was settling down. Young members of the royal family, Mbesi's siblings, were all seated in the high echelon section of the square. Traditionally events like this were informal, so attendants had the option to remain standing or take seats. "You two go and take your seats. I'll remain standing just to hear Inoni and then I'll proceed home."

Soon a makeshift master of ceremonies took the center stage to welcome everybody and introduce Inoni, the poetry singer.

Inoni had brought along with him two sidekicks, a *marimba* and a banjo (*kadete*) player who would softly play their instruments while he sang his poem. But to the surprise of everyone, particularly Saaka, Inoni had changed his mind and was going to sing a song with a message.

Isi yiswe igutawalaga, na madalaka
dugata na bayanda duchala gusoma,
gusoma, bagalangwa jikalile
nulu bagutumamaga, guleka
gudima ng'ombe, ng'ombe
jiding'we bakulumu,
imhanda majinji
habali singa
utum'untale
ubuhulu
mpaga
dutawale.

Badagi jagi kaya
mugabone ning'w-ubuluhi
mugayudaha na minzi
na mapilipili ng'wulima
ng'wolya ng'wululwa.

It was a song that mystified Saaka's mind. Somehow it seemed to echo Chief Manana's futuristic words and made him think of Inoni as a mystery man who had the ability to read people's minds and see the future.

Our land will soon be
independent of colonial
power. As we register to vote
let us send our boys to school
to learn the modern ways
and hold positions of office.
They should not look after cattle,
that's for the elderly to take care of.

Have we not heard our leader? Freedom,
freedom we must achieve.

Colonists, leave us alone.
You must learn to suffer as well as
learn to fetch your own water,
plant your own gardens,
grow your own chili,
eat it, and get burned.

As the audience cheerfully applauded, Inoni waved his hand and began to walk toward the exit. He wasn't quite past the gate when he saw Saaka standing, his arms folded across his chest with a stern look on his face. "S-s-so, Inoni, what a song you had this evening. Is this something you had planned or was it some mystical inspiration? I know that your poetry has always evolved around love, peace, and good rains . . . but never before have you ventured into politics." Perplexed by the coincidence of events, Saaka was curious to know whether Inoni had in him the extraordinary psychic power of knowing what another person was thinking–in this case, Chief Manana. "Master Saaka, you must understand that a poet is, in essence, a dreamer who remembers his dreams and tells them in words. And, as you know, dreams come in all sorts. They hardly have any boundaries or pattern. . . . What makes the boundaries and pattern is the decision of which dream to tell and which one to leave untold. What I sang tonight was an old dream, a dream that I had chosen not to tell because it would not have made any sense at the time. But tonight, I felt like it was the right moment and place to tell the dream as I looked at the crowd of our young men who are getting modern education. Yes, I was inspired to tell something that is outside the pattern of my poetry."

"I see," Saaka remarked. "I hope your dream manifests itself in a more peaceful and prosperous Izumba. You see, lately I have been observing change in some people's philosophy concerning the future of the country of which our dominion is a part, and certainly your song seemed to concur with these rather unconventional thoughts." He paused. "It frightens me, Inoni. Because once dominions lose their authenticity under the new sovereign government, which in my opinion will be fostered by the forces of the outgoing colonists, we shall simply become subjects under a new master. I am a traditionalist, I believe in natural causes. Let there be change when we are ready for change in the way nature dictates things. You see, the colonists have not been that bad after all. For one thing, they have honored customary laws and therefore retained chiefdoms as part of their government. Chief Manana and others have continued to lead their dominions with very little interruption. But who knows what may become of all this once the colonists are gone?"

"Your point is well taken, Master Saaka. But you must understand that before we can begin to exercise our originality, there has to be a step toward the freedom to do so, no matter how small that step may be. What you say is without question true. That although the colonists may leave the land they will always have a handle on the way our new government will run things. But at least we will have gained an important portion of our freedom. Otherwise, to let things go on the way they are and expect a natural transformation, we may never see the day of our being original in our way of thinking. You have heard the story of the man who tried to make a wooden bicycle and was severely reprimanded for doing so? That is what I mean by seeking the freedom to exercise original thinking. That man may have copied the idea of the bicycle as it looks today, but at least he had his own original thought of using wood."

Saaka listened in silence, perplexed by the depth of the poet's philosophy. "Master Saaka, I can see how deeply concerned you are about this impending phenomenal change. You fear for the loss of your personal esteem and all the privileges you have enjoyed over the years under Chief Manana. But perhaps this is the way toward an even better Izumba. If not for you and me, maybe our children's children."

As Inoni realized that the two of them had strolled down to the gates where each had to go his separate way, he decided to end the subject. "Master Saaka, as you can see it's getting late. I have to go and attend to ailing Gisamu," Inoni's favorite ox. "The boys don't know how to handle him well."

"Inoni," Saaka spoke after his long silence, "you are a man of many colors, and this is one I have not seen before. But let's just hope you are right. By the way, how is Gisamu doing?"

"Oh! You know Gisamu. He will pull through. He has improved greatly these last few days and I intend to keep him off the yoke the rest of this season."

"That's good to hear. Well, when he's fully recovered, bring him over, let him browse in the valley with my oxen and maybe they will rough him up a little to make him regain his full vitality. He will be a stranger to them, you know?"

"Not a bad idea, Master Saaka." The two men laughed, shook hands, and parted.

As Saaka approached home, he pondered, *It's now a matter of hours before a historical event takes place and yet I'm the only person who knows about it besides Chief Manana and Master Mbesi.* He wondered how Tunge, Chief Manana's first-born to the first wife, was going to take it once it was in the open. But contrary to his worries, Tunge would be aware of what was about to happen, for Chief Manana was a wise man. He had done the necessary protocol of informing his older son of what his intentions were concerning the transfer of power well ahead of time. You see, Chief Manana was a man who commanded respect and great power but at the same time he was a family man. He loved his children and grandchildren. It was not uncommon for him to show up at any of his children's homes within the compound, unannounced, to spend time with his grandchildren and chat with the son or daughter. And it was in this manner that one evening before the meeting with Mbesi was to take place, the chief had decided to visit Tunge's home, which was located in the east corner of the fifty-acre royal compound.

That evening Tunge had been home playing *Bao* with his son when he heard the sounds of galloping horses. Immediately he knew it was his father paying yet another unannounced visit.

"Where are my grandchildren? I've come to see them!" shouted Chief Manana as he walked toward Tunge.

"In the back yard," replied Tunge. "I don't think they are expecting you." He stood up and walked to meet his father. The two greeted each other in the customary manner in which the son bowed while holding his father's hand and placing the ring on the hand against his forehead. It was also customary that Tunge's wife and children would come forth to greet the chief. The two men then sat in the chairs under the canopy outside Tunge's house while Chief Manana's two sentries rode their horses in opposite directions to take positions of guard, giving the father and son privacy.

For a moment the two sat in silence, watching the sun as it slowly slunk away into the valley beyond Izumba hill. And while a gentle, cool breeze swept across the royal compound, the moment could not have been more perfect for father and son to sit down and discuss a matter as important as one that was on Chief Manana's mind.

"Tunge, my visit tonight is unlike the many visits I have made before, unannounced. This one is for a special purpose. I wanted to come and see you at a time when things had slowed down, and I'm pleased to find that you were in a relaxed mood, playing *Bao* with your son. By the way, how did things go at the meeting with the permit man?"

"I think we'll get the permit to begin buying the produce from the neighboring chiefdoms and shipping it across the borders. Next week our solicitor, Limbe, and I are going to meet with the representatives of our counterparts to agree on how the deal will benefit all sides. Limbe knows all the technicalities involved. He will have it all written down and papers will be signed. I will be there to make sure that our interests are well protected . . . after all, we are the ones with all the equipment and means of transportation. I was waiting for everything to be put together before presenting you with a full report."

"I understand, and I shouldn't have brought it up at this juncture. As you know, son, I have always been proud of you. I have never doubted you in whatever you do. You are a quiet but very clever man and that gives me great confidence in you. I know that much of the wealth we have amassed in the last two decades had come through your hand and I have no intention of taking that virtue away from you." Chief Manana paused for a moment while Tunge, who had been listening intently with his hands cupped together, suddenly lit up, looked at his father in the eye, and began to nod his head as though this was the first time he had ever heard his father say such words.

"Now, having said this," Chief Manana began, "I want you to listen very carefully. First I want you to look at me, and what do you see? I'm sure that what you see today is not what you saw ten or twenty years ago and certainly not what you will see in the next ten years. So you know as well as I do that some day, someone is going to have to step in my shoes. And traditionally, that is your 'birthright'. You are my first-born by my first wife. It goes without question that the next leader of Izumba would be you, after I am gone. But this is where the critical matter comes in and I will not object to your indignation if you should find my proposition inconsiderate and viciously denying you of your unquestionable right. My son, for the last month, I have been spending a number of hours in my private chambers pondering over something I should not do according to traditional norms. But I have come to terms with my conscience and have decided I am going to do it.

"Son, I have decided that when the time is right for me to relinquish the throne, your brother Mbesi will take my place. Meanwhile you, as guardian of the family's wealth, will continue to be in that honorable position. However, having said this, I am aware that you may find this to be most disturbing, humiliating, and even alienating . . . but, I have carefully thought this over and have convinced myself that the reasons behind my decision are humbly justifiable. I have looked at the way things are going today. Surely it's not the way it used to be in my days of youth and I think you'll agree with me that even in your teenage years things were different. You see, today there are people who are standing up to challenge the colonists and demand that we become independent of their rule. If this should come to pass, that we have our own sovereign government, nobody knows for sure that chiefdoms are going to be honored in the way the colonists have. You know colonists came in with their own style of governing . . . whereby the small grass-root governments are left undisturbed, which to me makes a lot of sense. You see, it is easier to speak to five people than it is to speak to ten and get your word heard.

"The new government may not follow the same style . . . and that is what worries me. Chiefs, if they are to remain in existence, will simply be government workers. That is why I have decided that Mbesi should be prepared for stepping in when it is time to make that change. Mbesi is an ambitious boy, but his ambitions are unlike yours. You want to build up wealth for the family and guard it for the benefit of your siblings, your children, and their children. Mbesi wants to read books and understand the ways of the colonists. He wants to drive cars and know how to repair them when they break down. He wants to have a bigger picture of how things work in the world and understand the modern ways of doing and making things. Well, if he can achieve all those things and be the leader of the people of Izumba, he will have a place in the new settings of government and his voice will be heard no matter what the form of rule may be.

"I intend to send him overseas where he can satisfy his quest for knowledge. That way he will be well prepared to take my place when it is time. I will inform your mother of this decision after I have discussed it with you."

"Father, you do not have to say much to try to convince me," Tunge began after a long silence. "I know my brother, he is a very intelligent young man and I think if you give him the opportunity to gain more modern knowledge he will be a good choice for your replacement. I will not cast blame on you for not giving me the same opportunity because I know that you did give me that chance when I was young, but I was not inclined to pursue it. At the time, I felt that the secondary school education that I received was more than enough for my needs and the family's needs. . . . You do remember the long talk we had when you had to ask me whether I wanted to continue with higher education?"

"Yes, indeed, I do," the chief quickly responded.

"My answer was, of course, no. I have not regretted that decision because it did not change you from being the same father that you have always been. The position that you have given me and the way you treat each and every one of my siblings gives me no reason to consider you an unreasonable father. My only concern, however, is how you are going to respond to the opinions of those who cherish tradition. I say this not in the remote sense of criticism nor defense of my rights. Rather I say it in defense of your own image before the eyes of the community and your peers."

Chief Manana took a deep breath, his eyes focused on the distant horizon. "Tunge," he began, "I am very happy to see that you are being open with me in expressing your views. That is a sign of wisdom and maturity. But I will say this; I have made this choice to make myself a sacrifice in a process of change, in that if the change I am trying to establish brings good results then someone is going to learn from it and embrace it as an example. If, on the other hand, it does not bring good results, then it will be a lesson to keep everyone from making the same choice."

As he paused, Chief Manana reached for the drink and poured some into Tunge's cup and then his. "Let us drink to peace, prosperity, and good heath. May *Liwelelo* (All Mighty) breathe upon you and your brother the breath of strength and wisdom."

After the drink, Tunge called for the guards and bade his father goodnight. Chief Manana went home with a sense of victory. He had won the support of his first-born son in his historical decision to pass the throne to the son of his second wife.

On the day of Chief Manana's meeting with Mbesi, Saaka, the chief of protocol, arrived earlier than usual at the royal palace private chambers to ensure that everything was in order according to the chief's instructions. The royal service staff looked magnificent as they set the table ready for the chief and the prince-to-be. Although nothing had been revealed to them as to the purpose of the occasion, it was obvious that an important event was about to happen and so they worked with a sense of curiosity to know what was in store for the day.

Meanwhile Ikeja, who had been assigned to prepare Mbesi's garments, wasted no time to attend to his special assignment and by noontime he had come to report to the chief of protocol that Master Mbesi's garments were ready. "Good," Saaka remarked. "Now I want you to go and fetch Master Mbesi's horse. Bring the horse and the garments to the quarters of Master Mbesi. Do not ride the horse."

"Master Saaka, will I be escorting Master Mbesi to someplace?" Ikeja frantically asked.

"You have not been instructed to do so but I will be more than happy to give you extra assignments if you so desire." Ikeja took off running as he saw the serious look on Saaka's face.

It was at this point that Saaka decided to go and meet Chief Manana in his other chamber to let him know that the special chamber was ready for the meeting and that Mbesi would be escorted to the meeting as scheduled. "I am looking forward to the meeting," Chief Manana remarked with a gleaming smile on his face. And with a hand gesture, he showed Saaka the way out to go and accompany the prince-to-be to the meeting.

The arrival of Mbesi at the royal palace in his warrior armor and in the company of the chief of protocol created a scene that was uncommon to many around the royal compound. It was a majestic arrival and Mbesi could not have looked better in his armor. Yet the attention he drew left the onlookers in a cloud of confusion at best. They marveled and whispered among themselves. "What is happening to Master Mbesi? We know he has once before appeared in his warrior armor, but it was a royal ceremony that was known to everyone well in advance.

"Maybe he is being crowned heir to the throne," a voice in the background was heard.

"Are you out of your mind? Mbesi could not be heir to the throne, we all know that. That is Tunge's right." Another voice echoed, "Maybe he is here to be congratulated for his recent athletic achievement." The discourse continued.

Meanwhile, inside the palace, Chief Manana was overwhelmed with pleasure to see his son looking so handsome in his armor. "Have a seat, my son." Chief Manana motioned his hand to show Mbesi his seat. "You look like a soldier who just won a battle, handsome and confident."

"But, Father, I still do not understand this whole proceeding. No one will tell me what it is all about, including Saaka," Mbesi asked before taking his seat.

"Well, son, relax. You have exercised patience for the last few days, so you should not begin to lose it now."

Saaka, who was quietly standing and observing the father and son talk, finally gestured to leave by bowing to the chief and the soon-to-be prince. What followed was a dialogue Chief Manana and his son Mbesi had never had before.

The chief started, "Mbesi, I am very happy that this day has finally come and I'm sure you are soon going to find it pleasing as well. As you may have gathered, the last two weeks have been very burdensome. My heart was troubled over the issue I am about to discuss with you. But after talking it over with your brother Tunge, my burden has been lifted. I feel delighted that I will be presenting to you a rightfully made decision. My son, I want you to understand that this is a historical moment because I am here to tell you that I have decided to make you the heir to the throne once my days are over. I know that this may sound to you as shocking news, but I am going to explain the matter in detail for you to understand why I made this decision."

'Father," Mbesi interrupted, "allow me to differ with you on this matter even before you elaborate on it. Is the throne not a birthright to my brother Tunge? And what could possibly change such a long-held tradition in the land of Izumba?"

"Very clever, young man!" applauded his father. "Of course, I expected you to ask that question and I'm happy you asked. You see, tradition is something that has always been good in our land for many, many years. But some things have been changing lately and they will continue to change as long as our ways of life are influenced by knowledge. Things that you young men are learning today are going to change the ways of life tomorrow. You see, today was yesterday's tomorrow, and I can speak of a yesterday that you do not know. You may find it hard to believe, for example, that in my days of youth we did not have the radio. But today you have the radio in almost every household. And the radio has now become the headman who addresses people, not in small numbers but in masses. People today are using knowledge to argue their point and make others to understand. That is why we even have those who are brave enough to face up to the colonizers and reason with them, saying we can govern ourselves as a nation if you give us the chance, and they are using knowledge to argue their point. In the old days, fear and taboo were guiding rods. People listened to their hearts because they were devoid of the universal knowledge that is available today. Now, because of these reasons, I have made the painful and unpopular decision to make you the heir of my throne. You will be a good blend in the bigger picture that is slowly unfolding."

Mbesi asked, "Father, is listening to your heart a bad thing?"

The chief responded, "No, it is not a bad thing. As a matter of fact, I should be asking you to listen to your heart because that is what I was taught when I was a young man. But I think, with the way we know things today, I must say it is not the heart that thinks, something that I would presume you are in a position to know even better because you are learning the bodily functions in school. I think the heart gives us signals when a thought process takes place in the head. So rather than going by the feeling in your heart, it is good to evaluate the thought that is in your head and make a prudent judgment. They say 'fear is man's worst enemy.' Yet, fear is always felt in the heart."

"I am going to need your wisdom if I'm to step in your shoes," said Mbesi.

"Yes," his father agreed, "but that will not be enough. You are going to need more education as well."

"Just to step aside from the subject, Father, when do you think this country is going to have its independence from the colonists?"

"That is an interesting question, because the answer may not be a simple one. We now have people who are seriously involved in the politics of independence and it would not surprise me if tomorrow the colonial governors got up and said it is time for us to leave and let you govern yourselves. That is how serious our politicians are at this time. But the main question is, how? How do we maintain our independence? The colonists know that they can leave us but we would still need them for many years to come. And until we have our own scientists, historians, and all those other experts who bring change in living conditions, we are going to continue being dependent in many ways. You must understand that all the countries in the world that are politically and economically independent have original thinkers who turned their thoughts into things that are useful in day-to-day life, such as bicycles, motorcars, airplanes, electricity, the radio, and many others that people use to save time and human energy.

Mbesi questioned, "Do you think that Izumba will one day have people like that?"

His father replied, "I believe that Izumba has such people. The only problem is that they have not discovered themselves for the simple reason that Izumba and the rest of Africa's 'clock of progress' was set back by the colonial rule, plus the fact that prior to the colonial era, people had no pressing need for a struggle to survive. Our weather conditions are not as extreme and our lands are fertile and filled with all kinds of fruit-bearing trees. As a result, there never was any real need for confronting nature for one's survival. But times are changing, the number of people in our land is rising, and the lands are becoming less fertile. Soon we are going to have to start thinking hard to find ways that will help us increase our productivity in the same way the colonizers did in their own lands. There is a saying, 'If you think hard enough, you'll find a solution.' That is why I want to send you abroad to go and learn the ways of those who have beat us in the game of progress. As soon as you have finished your high school curriculum here, I am sending you to a country of your choice for higher learning. That way, upon your return you will be fully prepared for your future position in Izumba."

"But, Father, you seem to be well aware of what the real problem of Izumba and the rest of Africa is. . . . Why haven't you made any effort to enlighten the people, or at least encourage them to be creative?"

"There is a starting point for everything in this world, Mbesi. Maybe this is how I want to initiate that effort, by giving you the opportunity to go and get higher education that you will use as a tool in your leadership. You see, I never had that opportunity. I have only learned things through what the English call 'the school of hard knocks.' I have learned by listening, observing, and, of course, the opportunity to travel extensively has helped me expand my level of imagination. But your leadership is going to be different. You will not only speak with wisdom but with knowledge as well. You will make others think and maybe elevate their sense of urgency to be creative."

Mbesi questioned further, "Do you think that the people of this land were creative before the arrival of the colonists?"

"Yes, of course. The people of Izumba were very creative," the chief replied. "You just have to look around and see some of the things that are still in use. The pottery, the iron farm implements–iron that was made from special river sand containing iron ore–hunting tools, the magnificent grass-thatched houses, and many other things that the indigenous people made for themselves. But it was at a different pace, a relatively slower pace. Again, just like I mentioned a moment ago, the natural environment posed no threat to their survival in terms of weather and food and, as a result, there was not struggle for survival. So when the colonists arrived, they saw a window of opportunity and infiltrated the economy of the land with their own things, made in their own homeland, meanwhile prohibiting the indigenous people from being creative. For example, a man once was severely punished for making a wooden bicycle. That sent a message across the land that any activity involving creative thinking meant risking one's life under the colonial rule.

"Consequently, an era of mental erosion set in and original thinking came to a standstill and became almost irrelevant in people's everyday life. You see, in my view, I think it takes only one generation to annihilate mentally, and you have reset the clock of creativity for generations to come. Therefore, knowingly or otherwise, the colonists became very successful in creating a generation of people filled with borrowed ideas. The young generations that have emerged are ones with a mind open only to acquired knowledge with no or very little originality. You are one of them, my son. That is why I want you to have at least a glimpse of the past that you can link with the future of this land when you become the leader. I have confidence that you are going to be the pivotal block of Izumba and the society at large, given the level of consciousness you have about real progress among the people of Africa."

"But, Father, where do you start when so many things have been introduced to us and we are accustomed to using them? No one wants to be bothered with the idea of originality," Mbesi argued.

"Sadly enough, that is true." His father agreed. "We have the cars, the lorries, the trains, and the household amenities that are obtainable as long as one has money. Nonetheless, you have to understand one thing. Those things cannot truly be our own despite acquiring them monetarily. The right to produce them rests in the hands of those who invented them. It is only when we are able to apply our talents in inventing the things that enhance our ability to produce goods and services that we can truly call them our own inasmuch as the right to produce, modify, market, and simply be proud of rests in our hands. Besides, I believe that a society becomes truly developed when its creative machinery is composed of its own people. But this will not come easily, certainly not as easily as it took us to lose it. It will be a lengthy process whose desired results may not be realized until generations to come. That means even though you may spearhead the reinvention of the wheel, as they call it, you may not be the beneficiary of your efforts, but rather your children and their children. However, your work will have created a hallmark in the history of Izumba and those around her. Remember, as a people, fully fledged with all the human traits, we have hopped on a fast-moving wagon without knowing where it takes us."

At this point, Mbesi sat in silence, his jaws and fists clenched. "We have got to regain our originality," he mumbled, his head shaking from side to side while staring at his hand-carved wooden wine tumbler as though this was the only thing he felt proud of.

Meanwhile, Chief Manana rose from his chair and slowly walked toward Mbesi and standing behind him, he reached out and placed his hand on his son's shoulder. "I am proud of you, my son. You seem to have the spirit that will turn you into a great leader." He then walked back to his chair and before he sat down, he held out his cup. "Let us drink to the great future of Izumba under your great leadership," Chief Manana said with a dignified smile on his face.

The meeting ended in a heightened consciousness of compatriotism rather than father and son as the two shook hands and embraced while reiterating words of courage and bravery.

Chapter Three

Preparation for Studies Abroad

During the period of preparation for his higher education abroad, Mbesi seemed to have undergone a phase of transformation both in mind and spirit. Within him the vision of a future Izumba became magnified. He saw himself as the leader of a people filled with new aspirations for the rebirth of original thinking and technology that would subsequently result in economic prosperity. As a central figure in the new Izumba political course aimed at the restoration of the fundamental human right to think creatively, he strongly believed that upon his return, he would play a remarkable role in the bigger national struggle for independence that was already in progress at the time. He was fully aware of the formidable challenges that lay ahead but he was determined to overcome them and become the man his father had envisioned.

By and large, the opportunity to pursue higher education could not have come at a better time. As Mbesi was on his way to graduating from high school, there was now an added motivation not only to complete his curriculum, but to be the best in the field of study he loved–mathematics. Mbesi had always dreamed of becoming a mathematician. It had been a dream of his since his early days of school as he always found great fascination in numbers. At one event, for example, the young man had been even more inspired when his father had been invited by the colonial district commissioner to officially inspect the local parade of the "KR" (King's Rifles), the name given to African soldiers enlisted in the colonial army. Mbesi, who had come along with his father, was fascinated to see the state of orderliness and discipline in the military environment. He admired the commander as a symbol of strong leadership. And in his young mind he had drawn a parallel between a military commander and a mathematician who had the discipline and skill to organize numbers to achieve a result. His father's offer, therefore, marked an important step toward realizing his dream.

Obviously, given his level of intellect, there was no doubt Mbesi would complete his high school program for admission to a higher learning institution abroad.

Meanwhile, Chief Manana wasted no time in ensuring that his son was going to the best school there was overseas. To begin with he consulted with friends of his among the colonial elite, explaining how he wanted his son to study abroad in the field of mathematics. And no sooner had contacts been made abroad numerous offers began to arrive for the prince to apply for admission. Furthermore, as the time was approaching, Chief Manana made sure that travel arrangements and living quarters were all in place before Mbesi's departure. The royal committee for entertainment was alerted for thorough preparations for Mbesi's high school graduation and going-away feast. Dignitaries–including chiefs from neighboring chiefdoms, local colonial district officials, Tunge's business acquaintances, community elders, and musicians were invited to attend the feast. All protocol details were carefully laid down, while the royal compound grounds were appropriately tended in readiness for the occasion.

A few days after the graduation and send-off celebration, Mbesi left his homeland for the first time in his life to go into a far-away land where he would engage in the pursuit of academic knowledge as well as study new cultures. Upon arrival at what was to be his home for the next several years, the young prince was amazed at the elaborate preparation for his reception by friends of his father. Obviously this was intended to treat Mbesi as a royal dignitary, thus making him feel at home almost immediately. But for Mbesi, it was a matter of honor to remain focused on his mission. He had his mind set to allow nothing that would detract from his goal. In his view he strongly believed that allowing himself an easy, luxurious lifestyle–which he was capable of, if he chose to–would be detrimental to his progress toward becoming a leader with a vision. For this reason he chose to be, from the outset, relentlessly determined in walking the narrow path toward his goal.

CHAPTER 4

Life in College

The early days of school for Mbesi were not easy. Unlike most of his classmates and other students in general, Mbesi had to deal with the adjustment factor in terms of his status as a royal personality, something that he could not easily keep concealed as long as there were people around him who knew who he was. His routine, therefore, became one that devoted less time to social events and leisure. Instead much of his after class time was spent in libraries and visiting museums and historical places. He socialized only where and when there was an opportunity to meet people from whom he could learn something of value. Needless to say, there was never a shortage of such opportunities as long as there were people with desires to establish relations with someone of his stature for speculative reasons.

In a manner of speaking, Mbesi's strategy of socializing seemed to work well. For while there were those who admired and considered him to be a potentially lucrative affiliate; he, too, was able to learn from them what he otherwise could not have learned in a classroom. Indeed, at times, Mbesi proved to be outright encumbered due to his relentless curiosity about almost everything ranging from simple to complex subjects. No sooner had the young prince become more acquainted with select personalities such as professors and other dignitaries who shared similar views over the issue of societal development did he find the opportunities invaluable. Through these associations Mbesi found a number of doors opening, including exclusive social functions, academic forums, and many such, both on campus and elsewhere, and often had the opportunity to make presentations or participate in discussions of substance.

With passage of time, a momentum of extra curriculum continued to build up around Mbesi to the extent that there was fear among close friends that his primary goal of pursuing a mathematics career was going to suffer. As they followed his trend of popularity and deepening involvement in matters of social disciplines they began to form a general consensus that Mbesi was following the wrong path. It had become obvious to them that Mbesi was a natural politician who only needed the tools that help shape a politician's career such as language, history, and law. But they couldn't have been further from the truth. Contrary to their popular belief, Mbesi continued to excel in his course work beyond everyone's imagination.

It is also important to point out at this juncture that while Mbesi exerted this rare effort to handle his school curriculum, there was yet another struggle going on in his mind. Indeed, one that may have been the main driving force behind everything he had wanted to achieve. As presented earlier in the discussion between Mbesi and his father, it had occurred to the young prince that the people of Izumba had been left behind in their economic development process owing, in some respect, to the circumstances imposed upon them by the colonists. This was even further reaffirmed in his view by the opportunity to travel and live in the colonist's homeland and observe the degree of disparity both technologically and economically between his homeland and the colonial masters' homeland. There was no doubt Izumba was well behind by any measure of development.

As a result, this impending unrest often inundated his mind with many unanswered questions. Time and again he had wondered to himself *Why us? When and how long before Izumba will come to grips with reality and begin to be the steward of her own ship?* Thus the energy and focus on accomplishing his goals.

In less time than was normal, Mbesi graduated with a bachelor's degree in science and immediately began to work on his master's degree in political science. He had a broad perspective in mind in the same way his father had envisioned and therefore did not mind sacrificing personal goals for the good of his community . More than ever before he felt that he had a moral obligation to rally the community and bring everyone's consciousness to the fact that Izumba needed creative minds to emerge from among them if indeed they wanted to be free of dependence upon the colonial masters. Hence the desire to arm himself with science and political background.

Suffice it to say that nothing changed in his campus lifestyle, if at all. He continued to be in the limelight of academia and politics, often traveling to make presentations or meet people interested in his cause. It would be unfair to omit what may be considered as a landmark in his school career when on one occasion, an invitation was extended to him by a panel of professors and members of the business community for an informal interview. This forum took place as a result of the charismatic persona that Mbesi had maintained both on campus and outside and to say the least, the fact that he was a prince who looked forward to becoming a future leader.

The setting was simple, in that questions were asked in a conversational format. There was no strict sequence of questions from among the members of the panel, nor was there a restriction against Mbesi from asking questions of his own. Many questions were asked and the young prince was gracious in his responses.

"Allow me to address you, Your Majesty, Prince Mbesi" one of the businessmen began.

"No, sir, you may simply call me Mbesi. After all, I am just a student under these circumstances. I feel more than honored to be in this forum."

"Thank you. I appreciate your humility, young man. Tell me, and I'm not trying to be facetious because I know very little about your culture. Do you have a faith in any supernatural being? The reason I pose this question to you is two-fold, one as a personal fortitude in the journey of life and beyond. Second, as a yardstick for social discipline."

"Yes, sir, I understand," Mbesi began, "and I must say that that is one of the very rare questions I have been asked. But I'll be happy to answer. Yes, I do, just like all human beings do. You see, I believe that all of us humans, unlike other living organisms, have a sense of our being, a conscious of our beginning and our destination; and together these senses lead us to the question of who our maker is. So, overtly or otherwise, we all have a faith in the cause of our being. However, because of interpretation and perception, we have religions, organized religions, one of which I happen to belong to as well."

"I understand that after your studies," Mbesi's professor of economics asked the next question, "you are going to be involved in the leadership of the people in your chiefdom, which I find to be ironic because you are a very brilliant young man who should pursue leadership at a much higher level."

"Thank you for the compliment, Dr. Peters. But I must say that although I am going to be in the role of leading people, politics is not my primary objective. Rather, I want to be in the role of enlightening people, a messenger, if you will. So regardless of the level at which I play this role, my main desire is to see that someone gets the message."

"What is your message?" Dr. Peters went on to ask.

"Creative thinking. This is the message I want to take to the people of Izumba and once it becomes fruitful in my homeland, I believe it will shed light to others around. I have chosen to take this cause to heart because I believe that the people of Izumba have the potential ability to develop technologies for the benefit of the land. As you know, the people of Africa in general have lagged behind technologically due to a number of reasons, and one that is most obvious is the climate and fertility of soils in different parts of the continent. The warm climate that presents no threat to life has allowed people to live without a pressing need for excessive struggle against nature. Therefore, even though there are tools and devices that they have developed, it has not been at a rate comparable to societies where the need to develop technology is key to the very survival of the people.

"Secondly, the adaptation to systems brought in by colonial rule has further weakened the indigenous people's ambition to be creative. But as times change and the possibility of independence becomes real, the African people are not only going to need strong political leadership but also a cultural fabric that embodies technology. And while it is true that technology can be acquired, I think and I believe that original creative thinking lays down a foundation upon which rudimentary technologies can develop and thrive. In a sense such an environment would allow the indigenous people to broaden their scope for finding solutions to their own problems and in the long run become contributors in a true sense to the global struggle for better conditions of living.

"In the short time I have lived in this land, I have studied much about the beginning of industrialization and found that simple inventions and discoveries are the reason for today's complex industrial system you have. I am sure that you as educators and business leaders pay much tribute to those who worked hard in developing their ideas to produce useful devices."

"Do you think that what you are articulating here, today, will be achieved within your lifetime?"

Dr. Sideburn, professor of political science, addressed his question to Mbesi.

"No, I do not think so because just like I mentioned earlier, technology must first be part of the culture of the people and I think that comes with time. The people have to first begin to realize that using firewood for fuel without alternatives leads to depletion of natural vegetation and forestry, which leads to depletion of soil fertility and lack of good rains. Once they realize that and begin to think on their own without expecting someone to think on their behalf of alternative solutions to the fuel problem, that is when technology begins to be part of the culture. But that will not take ten or twenty years. It may be much longer than that. What is important is that they embrace the concept as part of human nature and not simply a temporary phase. Again, that may take a long time that I may not live to enjoy the fruits of it. But my children and their children will."

Question after question, Mbesi seemed to be a young man with a sincere passion for real change among his people. He appealed to the educators and business leaders gathered to hear him that they were the shining lights not only within their homeland but to the world at large for having knowledge of the history of industrialization and technology. In addition, should they be inclined to support his cause, it should be through enlightening people on original creative thinking.

CHAPTER 5

Graduation and Return to Izumba

After four and a half years, Mbesi graduated with a master's degree in political science. It was an accomplishment he had strived for dearly, to fulfill in part his father's wish and his dream for the future of Izumba. On the day of his arrival in Izumba, he was met by family, friends, and fans from near and far. As he greeted a select group of the inner royal circle, an announcement was made to the rest of those who had come to meet the prince. "You may go home now," Saaka, the chief of protocol, began in a voice filled with exuberance. "His majesty the prince will need some time to rest. I want to thank you for coming to meet him and, just as much as you would like to speak with him, he is likewise eager to speak to you after the long period of absence. The day after tomorrow, at 10 A.M., there will be an assembly to which you are all invited. His majesty the prince will officially greet you and speak of his days in the foreign land. Following his majesty's speech, we will all celebrate his return. Bring your children and your empty bellies, there will be plenty of food for everyone. Be prepared to dance and sing in celebration of his majesty's return. May you go in peace."

Chief Manana, who was now in his late seventies, was overwhelmed with joy to see the day of his son's return. He had decided not to appear at the brief reception near the royal gate where everyone had gathered. Instead he chose to retreat to the special chamber where he had met with his son to discuss his dream of Izumba's future and grant to his son the honor to travel abroad and pursue knowledge for the benefit of Izumba. He had instructed Saaka to brief Mbesi of his desire to meet in private with his son for the first time in four and a half years. Saaka had wasted no time to inform Mbesi of the arrangement for meeting his father.

After the protocols of arrival and greetings, the two men strolled down to the royal palace where Mbesi would meet his father with utmost joy and excitement.

"Welcome, my son," the chief began as he gently rose from his chair with his arms open, ready to embrace his son. "I am thankful to the Almighty (*Liwelelo*) that you have returned safe and in good health. The photos you have sent over the years have been my greatest inspiration. I can tell you look more mature and dignified."

"I am glad to be back home, Father," Mbesi said as the two of them embraced. "I hope the burden of worrying about me has not been overbearing on your health."

"No, but your mother's worries were a bit overbearing. The family had to stand by me in keeping her assured that you were safe and would return to see her again."

At this time, Saaka excused himself after ushering two service personnel to come in and serve a beverage. The warm reunion of father and son seemed endless as they chatted and shared stories of a large variety, including Mbesi's experiences in the foreign land and the future that both of them looked forward to. But a scheduled evening dinner had to intercede, so the two had to join other members of the family and friends for the well-prepared welcoming feast.

Two days later. . . .

It couldn't have been a more perfect day for the anticipated gathering. The atmosphere was calm with clear skies and a gentle breeze sweeping across the undulating hills of Izumba. Attendants had begun to arrive well in the early hours of the day, securing tree-shaded areas in readiness to hear their future leader speak for the first time. As the hour approached, the air began to fill with a roaring sound of voices from the gathering multitudes of people. Around the stage upon which the prince would stand to deliver his speech, traditional dancers and musicians gathered, all eagerly awaiting to present their well-rehearsed performances.

At around quarter to eleven a senior royal official motioned to the crowd, calling for silence as Chief Manana, Mbesi, and a host of other dignitaries approached the stage to take their sitting positions.

But suddenly there was a loud sound of applause from the crowd followed by what seemed to be a pandemonium of music, cheering, chanting, and stage dances that sent a number of officials flying off their seats to try and bring the multitudes to order. The ensuing moment of silence finally gave the master of ceremonies the chance to give what was, indeed, the most elaborate introduction of the day's speaker, his majesty, the prince.

Chapter 6

The Speech

"My fellow citizens of Izumba, thank you for coming to share this joyous moment with me today. I am aware that this is a planting season when most of you have been spending the day's precious time in the fields. Your loyalty is greatly appreciated.

"Today is the beginning of a new chapter in the history of our beloved land. It is a new beginning because today we have gathered here with a desire to rekindle the flames of progress that our ancestors once carried around. With that in mind, therefore, I would like to begin by giving you an account of my long absence that lasted four and a half years. I will, however, try to be as brief as I possibly can because I understand that you have suspended your daily duties to which you must return with a new zeal.

"The last four and a half years of my stay aboard have been, in part, a period of acquiring academic knowledge and, in part, a time of observation. And I must say the latter has been the most rewarding experience. I cannot thank my father enough for his wisdom and courage in allowing me what has been an invaluable opportunity of seeking knowledge for the benefit of Izumba. Indeed, it gives me great pleasure to stand before you today to share my experiences with the hope that all of us will become inspired and determined to follow a course that leads to fundamental change in our way of life.

"Before I left for overseas, my father and I had a chance one day to sit down and have a lengthy conversation. I was much younger then with very little knowledge about realities of life. Despite the age factor, however, I was able to ask him as many questions as I could possibly think of, knowing he was my father. Some seemed childish while others were mature in context, enough to make him ponder before he could give an answer. As I recall, one of the difficult questions I asked him was why Izumba and her people and those around us lacked the ability to develop and produce our own labor-saving devices instead preferring to buy ones that are made from outside. His answer to my question became the key to my quest for knowledge and hope for a better Izumba.

"Once I had the privilege to be in the land where modern technology has thrived, I was brought to the realization that technology is a part and parcel of the culture of the people. The goods that reach us in the form we see them have, each, a unique history of their own; how it started, when it started, who created it, and a path of progression leading to the final form that we see and admire. From that point I was made to understand that it takes a great amount of time and discipline to develop anything of value to mankind. Societies that have excelled in technology, therefore, pride themselves over individuals who have gone through the painful process of inventing and developing a product that becomes useful to mankind. For in that process there may have been countless numbers of failures. But despite that, those individuals persevered and finally they achieved what they had in mind. I visited a number of historical sites where original designs of different devices and machinery were displayed and was amazed to see with my own eyes the enormous transformation that has taken place between the original prototypes and the present form, such as that of the lorry and passenger bus we see today.

"Ladies and gentlemen, the political independence that our country has achieved gives us the opportunity to begin building up a technological culture." (Political independence had been gained during Mbesi's absence and the indigenous government had maintained chiefdoms as part of its structural format of governance.) "I strongly believe that Izumba can be technologically and economically progressive. I believe this because at one point in the history of this land, our ancestors made their own tools and devised methods of providing for their livelihood. They worked hard, they were creative, and many were good tradesmen. You know, as we are assembled here today, that many communities living along the coast of the Indian

Ocean are comprised of many different tribes, including our own tribesmen who to this day speak our vernacular. They are there as a result of trade. Men and women who walked for over seven hundred miles carrying their own goods with which they would exchange for pearls and other goods from the coastal region. Occasionally, some would stay behind to establish a new life on the coast. But the majority of them returned home only to make yet more trips to the coast. This morning, as I look around, I still can see some of you wearing ornaments made by the very hands of those forefathers and mothers I speak about.

"Things changed when we began to adapt ourselves to things that were brought to us from outside, not made by us but which were made so readily available to us and in great abundance. We adapted ourselves to the monetary system that was not so prevalent before the arrival of the outside rule. We were directed in how to work for money and how to spend the money. Soon our innovative passions began to wither like a flower in an arid land. Our will was lost while our strengths were pawned to the currency made out of paper.

"Men and women of Izumba, brothers and sisters, mothers and fathers, I stand before you this morning to cast no blame on anyone but ourselves. We must remove the blindfold that has kept us from finding our way forward. We must not be complacent with the mere political independence that we have gained from the colonial masters. For that in itself alone is merely a key to the grounds of freedom that will allow us to make choices and decisions for what is good for us as communities and society at large. In essence, we must know and understand the true definition of independence, which I would like to illustrate by the following simple story.

"About seven years ago when I was in high school, there was a gathering of elders on one Saturday morning as we all know it to occur every so often in our community. And on that particular day I had a brief moment of conversation with one of the elders whose name I would like to keep unmentioned. During our conversation, he asked me a question that has ever since been my key cornerstone of focus. He asked me, 'How long has it been since you have been going to school?' My answer to his question was, 'Thirteen years.' 'That is quite a long time of learning,' he remarked. Then he went on to ask a secondary question, 'Do you now know how to make a needle?' My answer was, of course, 'No, sir, I do not know how to make a needle. They do not teach us that in school.' There was a pause between my answer and his next words. I could tell he was rather uncomfortable asking the next question. Nonetheless, with a bit of hesitation, he posed the final question: 'How can we then expect our young men and women to be useful to our community if you have not learned to make the smallest tool in life?' It was a logical question based on size. In his mind he must have thought that if we cannot make the smallest tool in life after all those years of learning, how long will it take to learn how to make the bigger things? That is a mind focused on technology. How ironic that it should come from someone who never went to a formal school as we know it today.

"The process of making a needle, from a modern technological standpoint, may not be as simple as he may have imagined. Nevertheless, he raised a challenging question to me and I believe the same will be a challenge to you this morning. You see, as my answer was to this noble man on that day, the statement that making needles was not taught in school stands to be true even to this day. Our school courses are not designed to make us become creative thinkers but rather to make us better users of knowledge and methods that have already been created and developed by others. You should not be surprised that this is true even in the countries where technology is advanced. Formal schools are meant to teach knowledge that has already been developed and assembled by another person.

"After spending four and a half years in the colonial master's land, I learned that some of the greatest inventors never spent many years in formal schools. Instead they spent time thinking, developing their ideas, and converting those ideas into tangible and useful things such as machines that make needles in large quantity.

"Ladies and gentlemen, the time is now that our culture begins to take a different course aimed at a future society filled with creative thinkers. A society of people who spent time thinking of ways of how to improve our quality of life in the same way our ancestors learned to tackle life by making tools for hunting, tilling the land, building shelters, clothing material, ornaments, and many other things that we know still exist to this day. We must prepare our youth to face this challenge and become enculturated to the ideal of original thinking.

"We must not delude ourselves, however, that by adapting a culture of original thinking we abandon the knowledge and skills we have acquired from the colonists. On the contrary, we must weave those threads of modernity into our fabric of progress. That is to say if the colonists taught us to add four and six to equal ten we must not change the result of those two numbers to something less or more than ten for the sake of being original. What the colonists have taught us is the art of organizing and assembling laws of nature which are universal. In a simple illustration, if you take a stick and break it in the middle, the result is two pieces equal in length. That result will be true here in Izumba as well as in Bangladesh, India. What is creative in this phenomenon is the assigning of symbols to represent the whole unit, that is the stick and the two pieces deriving from the breaking of the stick. Likewise, the result of joining the two pieces together would be equally the same regardless of location on the face of the Earth.

"Ladies and gentlemen, sons and daughters of Izumba, you must hear and understand me this morning. My contention and aspiration is not to impart dissension against the laws of nature and the universal knowledge that has been exposed to us. Instead, I am here to call upon each individual gifted with the properties of a human being to utilize the most precious property, the mind, in search for better and more efficient ways and means of performing tasks; be it in farming, building houses, preparing medicines, transportation, and many others. I believe and have confidence that we as a people can improve upon our traditional ways or discover alternatives to what we currently are used to. By so doing we will be creating a link between us and the rest of the world as others will want to exchange what they have for what we are able to produce skillfully and with perfection.

"Thank you, and may the spirit of *Liwelelo* (the Almighty) be upon our determination to utilize the gifts He has bestowed on us."

Reference List

Kagan, Donald; Frank M. Turner; and Steven Ozment. *Western Heritage: Early Nineteenth Century Industrialization. New York: Macmillan Publishing Co. 1983.*

Kenyatta, Jomo. *Facing Mt. Kenya. New York: Random House, Inc. 1965.*

Mazrui, Dr. A.A. Film Production. "The Africans: A Triple Heritage." Jointly produced by the BBC and WETA, 1986.